For Ferris & Ursula ~ T. L. • *For Jesse ~ L. C.*

First published 2020 by Walker Books Ltd, 87 Vauxhall Walk, London SE11 5HJ • Text © 2020 Tanya Landman • Illustrations © 2020 Laura Carlin •
The right of Tanya Landman and Laura Carlin to be identified as author and illustrator respectively of this work has been asserted by them in accordance
with the Copyright, Designs and Patents Act 1988 • This book has been typeset in Bembo • Printed in China • All rights reserved • 10 9 8 7 6 5 4 3 2 1
• No part of this book may be reproduced, transmitted or stored in an information retrieval system in any form or by any means, graphic, electronic
or mechanical, including photocopying, taping and recording, without prior written permission from the publisher • British Library Cataloguing
in Publication Data: a catalogue record for this book is available from the British Library • ISBN 978-1-4063-4939-9 • **www.walkerstudio.com**

The Song of the Nightingale

Tanya Landman • ILLUSTRATED BY *Laura* Carlin

WALKER ■ STUDIO

AN IMPRINT OF WALKER BOOKS

The earth was young and fresh and full of colour.

By day the golden sun hung in a clear blue sky.
Silvered streams ran down purple
mountains into deep green seas.

By night the moon lay on a quilt of velvet black, draped over snowcapped poles.

There were burning deserts of yellow and orange and flaming red. Shaded forests were filled with trees and flowers every colour of the rainbow.

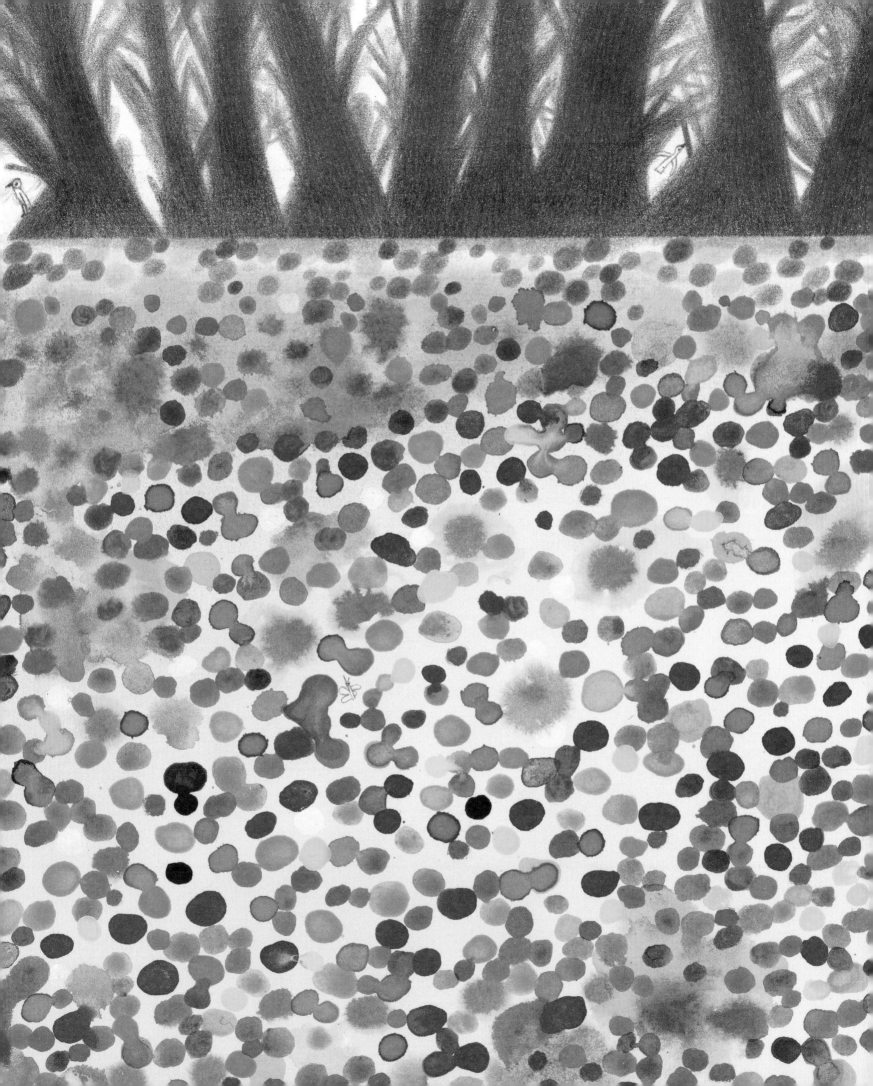

But the animals! They were dull and drab. And the painter had decided: SOMETHING MUST BE DONE.

She called all the animals
together: snakes with scales
and fish with tails and pigs
with bristly hair. Whales that
swam and deer that ran and birds
that soared through the air.
There were wings on the bat
and teeth on the rat and
claws on the grizzly bear.

The queue stretched as far as
she could see. It was going to
be a very long day. The painter
rolled up her sleeves, and
opened her paintbox.

She started with the fiddly, wriggly animals,
dabbing dots on ladybirds and spots
on butterflies.

As the morning went on she slicked stripes on zebras and painted pentagons on giraffes. She popped penguins into sharp suits, and furnished flamingos with feathers of delicate pink.

The sun was high in the sky
when the painter stopped to rest.
The penguins waddled away and
plopped into the deep dark seas.
Flamingos took to the air – a rosy
blush across the sky. While the
painter watched them, a mandrill
sat on her paintbox and ended up
with a very colourful bottom.

The painter went back to work. She'd had enough of fiddly, twiddly patterns so she got out her biggest paintbrush and some enormous pots of paint. She painted crocodiles green, and elephants grey; kangaroos red and orang-utans orange; lions yellow …

and whales blue.

Four birds kept arguing about which
of them had been painted the prettiest
colour. They squawked and shrieked
and bumped into each other. But their
paint was still wet so those four birds got
splashes of different colours all over them.

They became the parrots.

The painter worked all day; animal after animal after animal, until she came to the very last in the queue. It was a tiny beetle who had waited patiently for its turn. Because it had stood so quietly for so long the painter took out a tiny pot of gold paint, and that little beetle became the golden scarab.

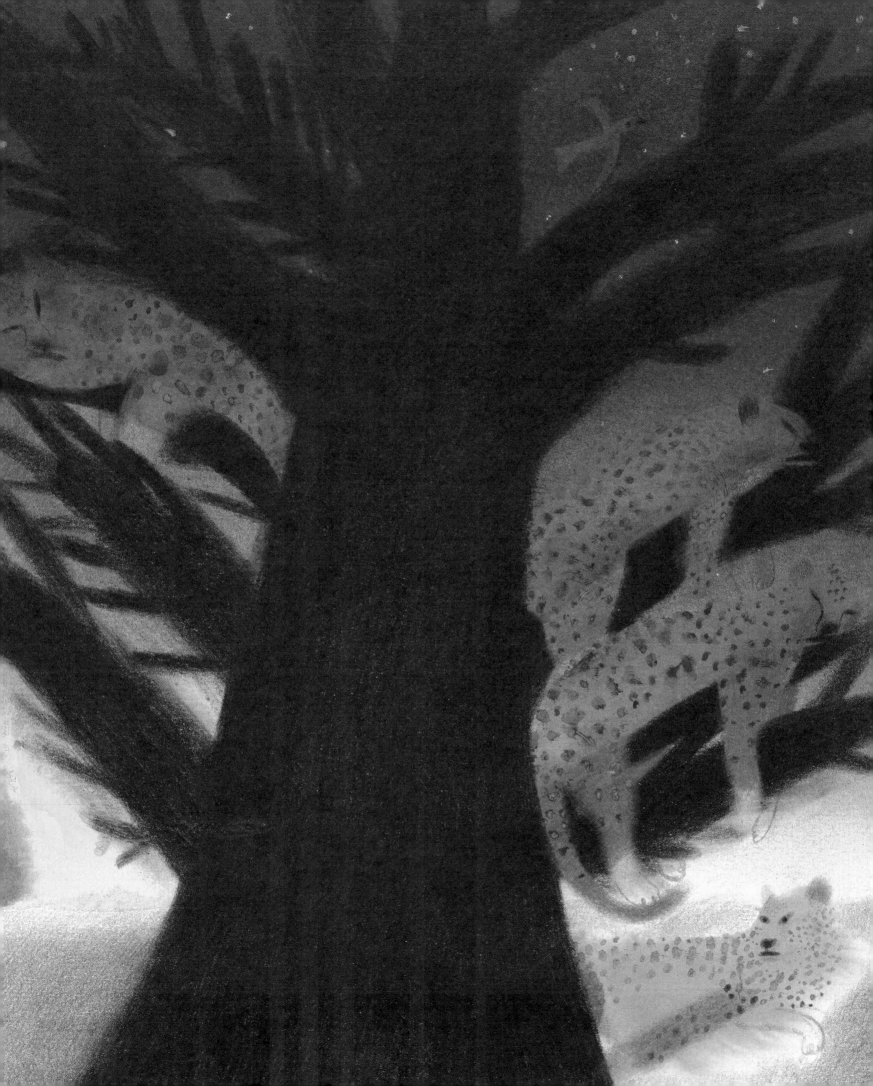

At last the job was done.

The sun was going down, and it was starting to get dark. The painter closed up her paintbox, and rolled down her sleeves.

She was just about to go home, when out of the shadows of the forest flew a little bird. It had been scared by the noise the animals had made as they queued to be painted and it didn't like the heat of the bright day. This bird preferred the coolness of evening and the stillness of night. It flew all the way up to the painter and perched on a branch, putting its head on one side and waiting to see what colour it would be.

The painter smiled, and opened her box. But there was no paint left! She had used all the colours on the other animals. There was nothing left for this little bird.

Then the painter looked at her brush. There on the tip – right on the very end – was a tiny drop of gold paint.

The painter asked the bird to open up its beak, and she put that drop of gold paint right at the back of its throat.

And then the painter asked the little bird to sing.

A stream of golden notes tumbled from its throat
and floated into the night. The song was so lovely
it brought tears of joy to the painter's eyes.

To this very day that little
bird prefers the coolness of
evening and the stillness
of night. When the sun
goes down and a velvety
darkness covers the earth it
comes out to sing with its
beautiful golden voice.

So we call that little bird the nightingale.